THOMAS & FRIENDS™

GO GO THOMAS!

Random House New York

Thomas the Tank Engine & Friends™

CREATED BY BRITT ALLCROFT

Based on The Railway Series by The Reverend W Awdry.

© 2013 Gullane (Thomas) LLC.

Thomas the Tank Engine & Friends and Thomas & Friends are trademarks of Gullane (Thomas) Limited.

HIT and the HIT Entertainment logo are trademarks of HIT Entertainment Limited.

randomhouse.com/kids   www.thomasandfriends.com

ISBN: 978-0-307-98216-2

MANUFACTURED IN CHINA   10 9 8 7 6 5 4 3 2 1

On the Island of Sodor, all the engines are very proud of their railway.
One morning, Sir Topham Hatt arrived at Tidmouth Sheds with a big book.
"Good morning, Sir!" Thomas peeped cheerfully.

"I have something to show you all," said Sir Topham. It was a book called *Great Railways,* and it was filled with photographs of mainland engines. The island engines whistled with wonder.

Sir Topham said a photographer was coming to take pictures for Sodor's very own *Great Railways* book.

"You all have jobs to do," he told the engines. "But don't delay. The photographer must leave by teatime."

The engines were excited about being photographed for the book.

"I'll be photographed because I'm the number-one tank engine," said Thomas.

"I will be photographed more," Gordon blustered, "because I'm fastest and best and pull the Express!" He puffed away grandly.

Thomas was cross.

As Thomas puffed off to his job at Farmer Trotter's farm, he decided to make sure that Gordon would *not* be photographed the most!

Soon after, Thomas saw Percy—and the photographer.

"If I hurry, I can be in Percy's picture," Thomas said to himself. He pumped his pistons and raced up to Percy . . . just as the camera flashed.

"Bye, Percy," said Thomas. "Flash, bang, wallop!"

Percy was so surprised that he crashed into a siding and then straight into a heap of coal! "Flatten my funnel!" he whistled.

But Thomas didn't see. He was too busy feeling pleased with himself.

As Thomas puffed through Maron Station, Gordon thundered by with the Express. "I'm sure Gordon hasn't been in a picture yet," Thomas said.

Farther down the track, Thomas found the photographer waiting to take a picture of James.

"If I *wheesh* and *whoosh*, I can be in James' photograph!" he thought.
He raced up to James . . . just as the camera flashed.

"Bye, James!" said Thomas. "Flash, bang, wallop!"

James was so surprised that he hit the buffers. His wheels bounced off
the track. "Rattle my rods!" he peeped.

Again, Thomas didn't notice. He was too busy feeling pleased with himself.

Thomas chuffed up to Farmer Trotter's just as Gordon steamed by.
"I've been in two magnificent photographs," Gordon said proudly.
Thomas' boiler bubbled. "I must find the photographer. If I hurry, I can
be in more pictures than Gordon!"

Thomas chuffed along, looking for the photographer. He saw him waiting to take a photograph of Henry, who was about to go through a tunnel.

Thomas raced toward the tunnel . . . just as Henry was huffing in. Thomas whistled, loud and long.

The photographer was so surprised that he dropped his camera
It crashed to the track, smashing to smithereens!

"My camera!" he cried. "The photographs are ruined!"

"Cinders and ashes!" Thomas gasped.

"What are you doing, Thomas?" Sir Topham Hatt asked, stepping down from Henry's cab.

Sir Topham Hatt told Thomas that Percy's mail trucks had derailed, James had hit the buffers—and now the camera was broken.

"I'm very sorry, Sir," Thomas said, explaining how he had raced to be in all the photographs. "Now none of us will be in any pictures, and it's my fault."

"I have another camera at Brendam Docks," the photographer said. "But there's no time to get it now."

"Yes, there is, sir. I'll bring it to you," said Thomas, and he raced away.

On his way back with the camera, Thomas saw Percy and James. Thomas apologized for what he'd done and promised to return to help them.

And with the assistance of Edward and Rocky, he did just that.

Later, when Gordon boasted that he'd been in more photographs, Thomas didn't mind at all. Helping his friends had been more important.

A few days later, Sir Topham Hatt called the engines to Knapford Station. The photographer was there, too.

"Here is the book of your railway," he said to Sir Topham.

When Thomas saw it, he gasped. The front cover showed a picture of Thomas and Rocky helping Percy!

"You and me, Percy!" Thomas said. "That's the best photograph of all!"

The Very Important Visitors enjoyed the party, balloons and all.
"Welcome to Sodor and to my railway," said Sir Topham. "Some of the
engines are really strong. Some are really fast. But they're all Really Useful!"
And Thomas and Gordon hooted and tooted happily.

"Gordon, you are fastest and best and you pull the Express," Thomas said. "Will you pick up the visitors?"

"Of course," Gordon replied. "Express coming through!"

Suddenly, Sir Topham Hatt realized that the party balloons had been left at Brendam Docks.

"I'll get them," Thomas said. "I may not be strong, but I'm *very* fast!"

Then Dowager Hatt stepped down from the train. "Where are my Very Important Visitors?" she asked.

"Looking at the Special Sights of Sodor," Thomas replied as everyone stared. He explained that he'd dropped off some of the visitors to lighten the carriages so he could pull the heavy Express.

Thomas arrived at Knapford Station for the welcome party.
Sir Topham was surprised to see him pulling the Express by himself.
"Why didn't you take Annie and Clarabel with you?" he asked.

He decided to leave some other visitors by a quiet field. They were puzzled. A cow in a field didn't seem like a Special Sight at all.

But Thomas was pleased. He now raced along with his lighter load.

Dowager Hatt didn't know that even more of her Very Important Visitors were no longer on the train.

Dowager Hatt didn't know that some of her visitors had been left behind.

As Thomas struggled to pull the heavy train, Gordon quickly approached.

"Hello, Gordon. Express coming through!" Thomas puffed. He knew the Express was still too heavy for him.

When it was time to go, Thomas and the Express slowly juddered away.
It was heavy—too heavy for Thomas. An idea popped into his pistons.

"I will leave some of the visitors to enjoy a Special Sight of Sodor. Then
the carriages will be lighter," he thought.

Thomas left some of the visitors at Blue Mountain Quarry, which didn't
seem like a Special Sight at all.

Thomas puffed and pulled. The Express was heavy.
He huffed heavily to the Sodor Search and Rescue Center.
Thomas' friends were surprised to see him pulling the Express.

Thomas invited Dowager Hatt aboard the Express.

Gordon glared. He was sure that Thomas was not strong enough to pull the Express.

Thomas disagreed. "I am Thomas, and I can pull the Express."

Sir Topham explained that Gordon would go to Misty Island to collect heavy cars of jobi wood. "I need a strong engine for the job," he said. "And you are very strong."

The visitors smiled at Gordon, who puffed proudly.

Sir Topham Hatt told Thomas to take Dowager Hatt and the visitors on a tour of the Special Sights of Sodor. "Afterward, you will bring them to Knapford Station for the party," he said.

"But Sir! I am Gordon, and I pull the Express!" Gordon gasped.

Thomas huffed huffily. "I am Thomas. I can pull the Express, too!" He smiled and raced away to Brendam Docks, where Dowager Hatt was welcoming the visitors.

Gordon steamed after Thomas.

"I hope Sir Topham Hatt asks me to show the visitors around the island," Thomas said.

"Sir Topham will ask *me*," said Gordon, sniffing snootily. "I am Gordon, and I pull the Express!"

It was a special day on the Island of Sodor.

Dowager Hatt was having a "Welcome to Sodor" party at Knapford Station for Very Important Visitors from the mainland.

There was much hustle and bustle. Thomas was excited.

THOMAS & FRIENDS™

Express Coming Through!

Random House 🏠 New York

Thomas the Tank Engine & Friends™

CREATED BY BRITT ALLCROFT

Based on The Railway Series by The Reverend W Awdry.
© 2013 Gullane (Thomas) LLC.

randomhouse.com/kids   www.thomasandfriends.com

ISBN: 978-0-307-98216-2

MANUFACTURED IN CHINA   10 9 8 7 6 5 4 3 2 1

HiT entertainment